Queen Vashti's Comfy Pants

By Leah Rachel Berkowitz

Illustrated by Ruth Bennett

APPLES & HONEY PRESS

For my mom, Amy, who sits in the front row for every Purim shpiel,
and in loving memory of my dad, David, whose gentle humor stole the show.
—LB

For my family, for supporting all my creative choices in life.
—RB

This book is a *midrash*, a story that elaborates on a narrative from the Bible, filling in the gaps and imagining how different characters might have felt in the moment. In this story, we start with an episode from the Book of Esther and imagine what might have really happened between Queen Vashti and the king.

The illustrations in this book were produced digitally using paintbrush textures.

Apples & Honey Press
An imprint of Behrman House Publishers
Millburn, New Jersey 07041
www.applesandhoneypress.com

ISBN 978-1-68115-563-0

Library of Congress Cataloging-in-Publication Data

Names: Berkowitz, Leah Rachel, 1981- author. | Bennett, Ruth (Illustrator), illustrator.
Title: Queen Vashti's comfy pants / by Leah Rachel Berkowitz ; illustrated by Ruth Bennett.
Description: Millburn, New Jersey : Apples & Honey Press, an imprint of Behrman House Publishers, [2021] | Audience: Grades K-1. | Summary: Queen Vashti is relaxing with her friends when the king demands that she dress up and entertain him and his friends, but she refuses, making him very angry. Includes author's note about the queens of Purim.
Identifiers: LCCN 2019057360 | ISBN 9781681155630 (hardback)
Subjects: LCSH: Vashti, Queen of Persia--Juvenile fiction. | CYAC: Stories in rhyme. | Vashti, Queen of Persia--Juvenile fiction. | Kings, queens, rulers, etc.--Fiction. | Bible. Old Testament--History of Biblical events--Fiction.
Classification: LCC PZ8.3.B4562 Que 2021 | DDC [E]--dc23
LC record available at https://lccn.loc.gov/2019057360

Design by Alexandra N. Segal
Edited by Dena Neusner
Art direction by Ann D. Koffsky
Printed in China
1 3 5 7 9 8 6 4 2

022138.4K1/B1635/A8

In her rumpus room Queen Vashti sat
in comfy pants and a funny hat.

She played gin rummy all night long
and sang her favorite silly song.

And all Queen Vashti's friends were there,
in comfy pants and braided hair.
They told Queen Vashti, one by one,
"We've never had quite **THIS MUCH FUN!**"

"How quiet it is, without the boys.
We're tired of their constant noise!
Today we're free from itchy dresses
and steering clear of
spills and messes!"

Meanwhile on the palace lawn,
the king had danced
from dusk 'til dawn.
His party had stretched on for days—
his mind was in a sugared haze.

And now his friends were bored and blue:
They'd plumb run out of things to do.
"We could play Wiffle Ball again,"
said all the king's advisers then.

The king stood up and said, "I know!
Let's make the queen put on a show!
Queen Vashti is just down the hall.
I'll send a messenger to call."

So just a little after four,
a knock rang out on Vashti's door.
The messenger declared, "I bring
an urgent message from the king."

"Queen Vashti must at once come down,
in her finest dress and royal crown,
and dance for all the king's good friends
until his royal party ends."

"NOW HOLD IT!" Vashti scolded.
"Freeze!
Could he at least say
'Thanks' or 'Please'?"
Queen Vashti found this very rude.
She did not like his attitude.

She told the messenger, "Please go
and tell the king that I said, 'NO.'
And if you could, please do explain:
I have my friends to entertain.

I will not don my royal crown
or change into a fancy gown.
I am not in the mood to dance,
for I am in my COMFY PANTS!"

The king was shocked to hear this news.
How could Queen Vashti dare refuse?
This was to him a crushing blow,
for no one ever told him, "NO!"

The king's friends sneered
and stood up straight:
"No king should have
to sit and wait!
Send word to Vashti's
room and say
she must come down
here **RIGHT AWAY**!"

'Make Vashti's friends come sing a tune,
and waltz beneath the harvest moon,

and pour our tea and bring us sweets,
while we recline on velvet seats!"

The messenger
crept down the hall
(he did not like this plan at all).
He gently knocked on Vashti's door
and whispered what the king asked for.

Queen Vashti answered, "Sir, please go,
and tell the king that I said, 'NO!
You cannot tell me what to do—
I'm royal, just as much as you!'"

The messenger slumped down the hall
and braced himself against the wall.

The king began to rage and fume
and marched himself to Vashti's room.

He pounded down
Queen Vashti's door
and stomped across
the marble floor.
The teacups trembled
on their tray,
but Vashti calmly
looked away.

"You must come dance," the monarch cried.
His face burned red with wounded pride.
"And I DEMAND your friends come, too,
or I'll make mincemeat out of you!"

The queen's friends stood and hollered, "**NO**!
We're happy here, and we won't go.
We are not in the mood to dance,
for we are in our **COMFY PANTS**!"

The king's face twisted in a frown.
"You're done here if you don't come down.
Have you forgotten who I am?
Your choice is simple:
dance . . . or **SCRAM!**"

Queen Vashti said, "Then that is that,"
and tipped the brim of her funny hat.
"You cannot tell us what to do,
so King, I think
we're done with you!"

Queen Vashti took her
suitcase down.
She packed her jewels
and royal crown,
and sturdy shoes,
and potted plants,
and seven pairs of
comfy pants.

She told her friends,
"Please, come with me:
There's so much world out there to see."
Her friends responded, one by one,
"Together, we'll have so much fun!"

So just a little
after eight,
the women stormed
the palace gate.
They left without
a backward glance—

to conquer the world in their comfy pants!

Dear Reader,

There are two queens in the story of Purim: Esther and Vashti. When I was a little girl, I always wanted to be Queen Esther, the beautiful and brave young girl who won the king's heart and pleaded with him to save the Jewish people. As a grown-up, I began to also appreciate Queen Vashti, who stood up for herself and said "No!" to the king's demands, even when it meant getting sent away. When do you feel more like Esther? When do you feel more like Vashti?

Although in the Bible it doesn't say why Vashti refused the king, this story imagines that it was because she had her own ideas about what to wear and how to have fun. When have you wanted to do something different from what everyone else wanted you to do? When have you stood up for yourself, and when have you gone along with the crowd? Why is it sometimes hard to be different?

Warmly,

Leah